a novella

WHAT DARKNESS CREEPS THROUGH

JASMINE CLARK

© What Darkness Creeps Through

A novella by Jasmine Clark

What Darkness Creeps Through is a work of fiction. Any character, event, or place is part of the author's imagination or used fictitiously.

Copyright © 2022 Jasmine Clark
All rights reserved.
Published in the United States of America.
ISBN: 979-8-218-10491-7

1. General Fiction. 2. Cosmic Horror. 3. Short Stories. 4. Eldritch Horror

Library of Congress Cataloging-in-Publication Data
Clark, Jasmine.
What Darkness Creeps Through: a novella/Jasmine Clark.

Printed in the United States of America

Cover art by Stefan Koidl

As the day fades, night takes shape. From the eyes you can't see, and fear you can't quite place. Moments staring into the abyss of dread as you notice what darkness creeps through.

CHAPTER 1

THE TEACHER

As soon as she crossed the threshold, it felt wrong. She could chalk it up to that day old coffee she drank on the way there, but no, something else felt off.

The air smelled the same. Pine and dirty water stung her nose. The same it always was in the morning. Quiet and somber. Her feet were so loud it made her nervous. Odd feelings and anxiety, boy, was this one of those mornings? The weather was beginning to fade from its harsh summer to an angelic fall. She should be thankful. After all, cooler weather meant chilled rooms. Her students would like that.

Ms. Thomlin was her name and every one of her coworkers called her Tommy. It was weird at first, people calling her such a nickname. Then again, it only meant she was officially apart of their realm — the realm of teachers. Like some pack of cool kids with their own code. Funny enough she never felt apart of any group. Always by her lonesome until she got this job. Working at a small school and teaching bright eyed first graders.

She loved her job, at least until today. That odd feeling lingered since she walked through the front door. Was she forgetting something? A conference, a lesson, a birthday? Maybe this was her body's way of alerting her to some misplaced thought she ought to figure out before the day began. Whatever it was, it soon became a pest. She stopped right there in the middle of the hallway and shook her head. Better to force the feeling off like some dog ridding itself from wet fur.

"Tommy, you okay?"

Frozen and quite embarrassed, she saw Mr. Kim. He looked on in puzzled fascination. She just couldn't tell if he were surprised by her behavior or amused. Then he smiled and all was right.

"I'm having one of those days Kim," she said, half lying, half confused herself.

"I see… Well, when you get a chance, there are forms you have to fill out for the trip for next month," he said, then walked off shaking his head. So he was amused.

Crap! The trip! There it was, reminded for her by the great Kim! She picked up her feet and jetted to her room. Inside, the room smelled putrid. It actually made her gasp. Of all the days, there just had to be a rat or something else unholy here. Maybe if she could hold her breath and find the papers, she could fill them out in the teacher's lounge. Right. Standing outside her room she took the biggest gulp of air and ran inside. Surely if the great Kim saw her now he'd be shaking his head at her again.

The teacher's lounge was pretty big, about the same size of her room. Out of all the schools in the district, theirs was the largest. And it was empty! Normally there'd be someone, or two, getting coffee, or making copies. Today must be one of those days for them too, she thought. She sat by the window and fanned out her paperwork. This could take several minutes, or longer if she messed up. How could she forget! While sitting and hovering her pen over the paper, she tried to remember when she had last heard about the trip. Funny, the memory was gone. Zapped and buffed out of her mind. Was there a trip? Well, she had been told of it by Mr. Kim, and she had the forms in her room, but…that nagging feeling again. That smell!

The putrid from her room was seeping into the one she was currently residing. Ugh, not this and not today. She went to the phone to call for the custodian. She hoped he was there, and not taking a smoke break. Not that he could on school grounds, but then again, no one was here. The school itself was located far into the crevice of the town, right on the line of the woods. The parking lot was the only space, besides the school, without trees. Oh, and the playground.

No answer. Right. Well, she could hold her breath to get this paperwork done. The idea of sitting in a room filling with yuck air was none too pleasing, but time was tick tick ticking away. Okay, one, two, three, hold. Somehow she was able to manage most of it until her gut clenched and she gagged. While still gasping from holding her breath too long, she rose to get ready to run to another room. From there she sprinted to Mr. Kim's class.

"Tommy!" he said, part enthusiastic and part befuddled.

"Sorry, can I borrow your room?" she asked, still gasping from her labored breaths.

"You good?"

"Yeah, just having one of those days."

"Well, my room is yours."

She sat at a desk by the window. The toy thing was cramped, but served its purpose.

"Done!" she exclaimed.

"Alright, see you later then," said Mr. Kim, this time smiling, no confusion to spot.

She walked to the custodian's room and saw he wasn't there. Checking her watch, it was almost seven thirty! She had about thirty more minutes, but her room, along with the lounge, was ripe with that putrid nonsense. Where was he?

She folded her arms and thought. Well, he is the custodian, maybe he's in the basement. So there she went.

Standing by the top step, the door was already open. The darkness lingered from below. A cool feeling slid its way up her spine, creating gooseflesh on her arms and legs. She rubbed her hands and thought for a moment. Checking her watch again, five minutes had passed. Damn, she was going to have to find this man or risk sitting in a class full of first graders whining about that smell. The latter was just as awful as that assault on her nose.

"Mr. Koch!" she yelled.

She didn't mean for her voice to project so loud, so harsh. But she was in a hurry and time was most important. Nothing, not even a tremor of steps. So she called to him again. By the third time she didn't care if she sounded like a bitch. Where was this man? Her watch said she had about fifteen minutes left. Now she had to pee. Walking away she heard a noise. It was faint, so it could have been anything, but it gave her that off feeling again. Looking into the darkness, she willed her eyes to see something. The longer she looked, the harder it was for her to see. She looked away to leave, but her vision was indeed getting worse. Wow, how hard did she strain her eyes? Or was she sleepy? That off feeling turned into dull sensation that radiated through her toes, head, and fingers. She felt herself going limp, then, nothing.

"Ms. Thomlin!" screamed a squeaky voiced youth.

She was looking at one of her students. His eyes stared intently at her as she blinked back a few times. It felt like a dream, almost.

"Ms. Thomlin, are you okay?" he asked.

The sweet faced boy waved his hand over her face to help snap her out of whatever. She was so confused, yet oddly, felt normal. It was as if she lost hours of her life, but things were just fine. She looked back at the boy again and stood.

"I'm fine," she said as she patted his red hair. It seemed awfully redder today. Or maybe she was just being ridiculous.

The students were going about talking, putting their things away, and some were already sitting on the rug to begin the morning meeting. She looked around. If this were a dream, then it was pretty damn vivid. Some of her dreams in the past had been detailed, but never this clear. Looking at the room, she counted all of her students. Even the red haired boy, who stood next to her and looked up with focused eyes. He smiled and she noticed his teeth. She could have sworn he lost a few some days ago.

During the morning meeting she went through the motions until she caught a whiff of that putrid smell. That smell! It was here this morning. This morning? She looked at her watch, eight fifteen. The students were quiet and waiting for her to get going. They were sweet kids, always well mannered, even for six year olds. Still, it wasn't right, something wasn't right. Her breath became heady like she was gearing for something. Another whiff and she was certain the rest of them smelled it, the putrid. She gagged and noticed their faces were less detailed. So was this a dream? Why was the disgusting scent so strong? Why couldn't she properly see their faces?

"Ms. Thomlin!" screamed one of the children.

The freckled child was trying to hide from the man. Tommy found herself standing and watching from the other side of the room. Her grip on reality was fading fast and now there was all this chaos. A man had entered the room and was brandishing an axe. Several students were on the floor, soaked in globs of blood. Tommy screamed too. The man continued toward the freckled child as if her screams were unheard. Eyeing the room she quickly saw another student hiding under a desk. The red haired boy.

"I'll kill all of you! You, you, monster!" said the man.

Before she even knew she was doing it, she ran over to him with a chair. For such a small thing, it made quite the impact on his head, denting his skull. Over and over she continued her assault until he lay lifeless on the floor. Her moment of strength waded, and now she was a trembling mess. With tears soaking her face, she noticed that this was no stranger, but a father of one of her students, one of the dead ones strewn somewhere in this very class. Had he killed them while she stood frozen for however many minutes?

The red haired boy ran over to her and buried his head in her side. She looked over at the freckled child and reached out a hand to let her know it was now safe. Either way, both of these children, including Tommy herself, would need years of therapy after this!

As they tried to settle into the aftermath of this horrible event, she heard more voices from the hall, heated voices. With both children on either side, she made her way to the door and took a peak. A man, another parent of the school, was holding a gun staring down five children. He was too far away that if she had tried to lunge toward him, he'd see her and shoot her down. Then there'd be seven dead children, the ones he had coward on the floor, and the two with her. What was happening? Why was this happening?

All around, there were a few bodies, but no sign of any other teacher. Where were they? What about the cops? She closed the door gently to not alert the crazed lunatic in the hall. The red haired boy whispered that he wanted to leave. The girl echoed his thoughts. The voices were flickering through her mind like a flurry of snowflakes on a winter night. Tommy thought franticly until she considered an escape. The only way out was the window, but her's led to the woods. Her car, which was now her goal, was in the lot. If she ran out her window, she'd have to run for it with two frightened children and however many lunatics waiting in the brush. It was too dangerous. So she thought about another idea, possibly a stupid one. The teacher's lounge.

Kneeling down, she made direct eye contact with the children, and in a quiet voice explained what they were going to do. The children were scared, but listened without question. They were shockingly calm. Grabbing their jackets, she got them ready for their daring escape. After pocketing her keys, she peaked outside her door. The man was still there. With a tearful eye, she saw as he fired his gun. For some odd reason, their deaths didn't register as a normal gunshot blast. Her vision blurred like some censored thing she might see on television. Then she noticed he was reloading. This was her moment, and it was now, or be shot.

From her class to the lounge, it only should have taken several seconds. It felt longer, more clumsy, more worried. When she saw the door, a heavy feeling of doubt hit her mind. What if there was another parent on the other side of that door? She should have brought a weapon, like a pair of scissors. It didn't matter because the room was empty. The chaos must have been during the morning before any specials started, otherwise there'd be someone here. Or maybe they were hiding. She shook her head and tried not to think of what ifs at this perilous time.

Slamming the door, she knew it was only a matter of seconds before the man came. So she locked it by placing a chair under the handle. Racing against her literal death, she had both of the kids by the hand as she clambered to the window. After lifting each child up and practically pushing them outside, she barely exited before she saw the man had already shot the door and was pushing his way inside!

Just like she had planned, the lounge led straight to the lot. The three ran toward her car while taking cover in case there were anymore weapon wielding nut jobs. When they made it to her vehicle, she used the key to open the door. She was too afraid to use the button and risk making a sound to alert anyone of their presence. Although, she felt that gun toting parent was on his way here regardless. Once the children were inside the backseat, she ordered them to put their seat belts on themselves. There was just no time to properly put them in like an adult should.

Her adrenaline must have been potent because she hadn't realized she was bleeding from her waist. Or was she shot? It was hard to tell, but there was no time for this, she had to leave. Boy was this a day! Driving out she peered into her rear window and saw the man running in the distance. It was hard to tell if it was the parent with the gun, or another one of the many psychos who were killing children! As her car went on hastily away from the school, she had a sudden feeling that something was odd. Then she remembered that same thing when she first entered the building in the morning. Somehow her memories were coming back, sort of. Darkness overtook the sky. What time was it really?

"Where are we going?" asked one of the children. She couldn't be sure who said that since their voices were not distinct.

It had broken her thoughts, so she stammered to come up with a lie. Something easy and a way to calm them. How the hell can she calm them from something like this? The whole mess was utterly strange. Even their escape seemed too implausible. She should have hid in the closet like the procedures dictated. In a drill that would have made sense, but this was real life! Somehow she did the complete opposite of her training. Stupid and foolish, but now she was escaping peril.

"Ms. Thomlin?" asked whoever.

Damn. Caught in another bout of thoughts.

"We are going to get help!" she said.

Honestly, if the parents were deranged, she feared what the other locals might be like. Was there some type of chemical or crisis causing this? And how many were affected? She should have brought her phone! Another lapse in judgement. Her waist really hurt. Maybe if she left the town completely, she'd find someone normal. No point in staying in a place that was far gone. So she drove, but only side streets incase the main ones were full of nuts.

It was much darker than before, and she wasn't sure how many hours had gone. The gas tank was nearing empty and she was still an hour away from her friend. He would know what to do; being from the military and all. Looking at her mirror, she tried to see the children's faces. They were so quiet it almost seemed like they weren't there. Darkness, she couldn't see. Safe to assume they got some rest. She had to stop by a station and find a phone. A way to reach her friend.

Lights shown in the distance. A gas station. Pulling in she stopped next to a pump. There was a man there, in army gear. For a moment, fear crept up to her, inflating her senses. Was he going to kill them? There wasn't any weapon she could see, and she did look pretty hard. Her car was practically empty, so driving off was not even a real option at this point. She opened the door and slowly made her way out. Walking to the man she noticed a familiar lingering smell, the putrid! Why was this smell following her! It was growing in intensity. The man hadn't gone closer. If anything, he was backing away.

She thought about getting into the car and leaving, even if it meant only going a fraction of a few feet. That smell! The man was waving her over and asking for her to get away from the car. Was this a ploy to separate her from the children? Was he going to kill them like that parent did to her students? She shook her head no and proceeded to get into the car. To her shock, the putrid was coming from the car. It was more severe and actually made her stand back a few feet. How could she abandon the children. Something urged her to go back to them, but that smell!

Before she knew it something had grabbed her. It was the man in the army gear. She looked up to make eye contact, and to curse him out, but she couldn't see his eyes. They were hidden under a mask, a gas mask! His entire get up was an army hazmat suit. Another man was shouting in the distance. It was hard to tell what was happening, but she might have heard, "don't get close to the car! Stop touching her!".

He was pulling her away as that person in the distance continued shouting. She wanted to resist him, but he was so strong. Whatever had started, whatever she was trying to run from, she had lost and he was taking her away. She looked over to her car with the kids. Then to her horror, a massive flame started pounding the car! Another army man had a flamethrower, entombing the children inside. The flame was so bright, so extreme, that it illuminated the vehicle. As she peered into the car to see them, it wasn't them. Something slimy, arms, or tentacles extending. The world around her was losing its shine and now she saw moss. It wasn't like normal moss from nature, but something new, translucent.

The car itself was caked in some brownish residue. It appeared grainy like ground up coffee. While processing this, she was thrust around to make sort of eye contact with the army man. He was talking, but she found it hard to listen. The smell was so incredible she felt herself going, leaving mentally. Her waist hurt a lot. He was now looking to the side, talking to someone? The other man with the flame thrower was pointing to something. To her, but down. Looking, she saw her side for the first time since she left the school. It wasn't blood. Maybe something squishy or even wet smooth. Whatever it was, it was going in, the hurt continued.

Making sort of eye contact again, she was pushed away, violently. The flamethrower was aimed at her. The army man that had held her earlier was trying to stop the other one. She fell hard, almost like her body lost all sense of function at once. The car was a blaze, but she couldn't see, the world was dark. Voices lingered, and then, nothing.

CHAPTER 2

THE CHAPERONE

A Saturday night. Supposed to be fun, but things went left as soon as it started. Mishca was on her way out of town when her cousin insisted on dragging her to a house party. Apparently, her parents wouldn't let her go without some form of supervision. It was their way of stopping her, because what teen wants to bring a boring adult to an adolescent party? Guess that was wishful thinking, because her cousin didn't mind a thirty something year old going.

They had been close for years, even as the then girl became an adolescent. Mishca was glad she still wanted to be around her, but still, she had wanted to leave town. It was going to be her big break, a way to really get into the industry. Her dream of becoming a music producer. Her parents had disagreed since forever and forced her to go to college for a real career. She had, but that didn't last. Soon she found her way out of college and out of her familial home. The decision was her big moment at the time, but the consequences were rough. She had no place to go and not enough buzz around her name to make a living. Into her uncle's home she went where she continued her bond with her little cousin.

Now that years had gone and she was finally making traction, she was ready to move on, make her dreams a profitable reality. Only, she had to chaperone for one last night.

Her cousin had put on her finest duds to turn heads at this party, but before getting there, she met up with her friends at the park. It should have been a quick meet up, but these were teens and they were utterly reckless. One of her friends thought it'd be a great idea to stand on a large rock and jump off. It was supposed to be a cool picture with all of them showing off their crew. Since it had rained earlier in the day, it was obvious the rock was slick. So when they all climbed up to make the jump, her cousin was the unfortunate one to reap the benefits of stupidity.

Mishca had been in her car and scrolling through her phone when she heard the scream. Not sure how, but she knew it was her cousin. Running fast, she saw the girl on the ground, her friends standing around like morons not knowing what to do. Cradling the girl, she looked her over.

"My arm," she said.

It was almost calm, like she was trying not to let the others know she was in pain. Mishca took her to the car when one of the friends asked about the party. The girl was taller than the rest, and thinner. Probably the leader of the pack.

"I'm taking her to the doctor. Find another way there. Or come with us," said Mishca.

It was harsh, harsher than she had meant, but the feeling went away. This was family. The tall girl stood with her arms folded. The others looked back and forth, trying to figure out what to do next. Only two of her cousin's friends came along, leaving two behind.

Fifteen minutes later and they were at the single level building. It was situated out in the industrial area where only businesses resided. With little to no traffic, it seemed desolate, even abandoned. The small town had this off kilter like hospital clinic place, but the real hospital that Mishca was use to was in a different town about thirty minutes away. As they drove into the lot they saw a few other cars. This meant that other patients were there, and her last night was going to be a long one.

After checking in, they all sat in the waiting room. It was small, just after the entrance. The nurses' station was to the left when you first walked in and enclosed behind a half wall and sliding glass. The actual area where patients were seen was to the right of the entrance through double doors. They were closed. For such a small out of the way place, it was surprisingly modern. The chairs were wood with pinkish plastic seats. The walls were a muted pink and a few plants were placed in the corners. On one of the walls was an elevated television; flat screen too.

Mishca took a look at the people in the room. A man with a woman, not sure who was the patient. Someone coughed, an elderly woman with a younger woman. A little boy with wild red hair and a chubby woman going through her purse and a handful of others she didn't care to glance at in the moment. She looked to her left to see her cousin sitting solemn. Two of her friends who had come with them were sitting off in the back by the window. They were looking for an outlet to play on their phone. Guess they regretted their decision to stay. Her cousin kept her head down and holding her wrist.

"Some night," the girl said.

"I guess," Mishca responded.

"What did my parents say?" she asked.

Mishca hadn't called them. In all the fuss, she forgot.

"I'll call them now," said Mishca.

"No, not yet. I just…I don't want to deal with them right now," she said.

Mishca understood. Without explanation, they agreed silently. It was their way, their bond over the years. At least for now, she wouldn't tell her aunt and uncle. She'd wait until the teen was with the doctor.

Twenty minutes came and went with no movement in the room. She looked at the nurses' station and the urge to ask was strong. No, she'd wait, she had to, for now. The others in the room were waiting silently, maybe a few murmurs here and there, but it was rather quiet. She wasn't sure when, but the television had lost reception. The other girls had sat on the row of seats next to her cousin. Boredom can ease any situation. It had made her cousin a bit more chatty. Guess it was easier to forget such an awful situation by distracting oneself. At least they had each other. Without the television, Mishca was pretty bored. The urge to go to the nurses' station had won and she got up.

"Hey," Mishca said as she knocked on the sliding glass partition.

It opened, squeaking all the way. The nurse was young, maybe mid twenties and cute. Not quite Mishca's type, but close enough. She had almost made a pass when she remembered that she was leaving town the next day. The kind young woman said they were swamped and that the doctors were very busy in the other side of the building. She meant the other side of the double doors.

"How long do you think," said Mishca, trying a flirty grin.

Talking to women was not exactly easy for her but she wanted to try. If she'd embarrassed herself then who cares, she wouldn't be in the town after tonight anyway.

"I can call, but… okay I'll call, give me a minute," she said back. There was no smile.

Mishca stood there watching as the woman made the call. Her face went from vacant, to disturbed. She looked over at another nurse who was filing papers.

"Sue, can you listen to this?"

The annoyance in her face as she put down the file was apparent. She came over reluctantly and took the phone. Once it was up to her ear, her eyes rang of shock and confusion. The woman, named Sue, decided to investigate. The other nurse looked up and seemed surprised to see Mishca still there. Insisting that everything was okay, she asked Mishca to sit and closed the partition quickly.

That was odd, Mishca thought. She walked back to the row of seats. All the while she eyed the nurse named Sue go beyond the double doors. As they opened a loud scream was heard. It didn't seem close, like it was further inside. The sound must have been so loud that it permeated the waiting room once the double doors were ajar. Everyone looked almost immediately in silence. Even the teens ended their ramblings to take notice.

"What do you think that was?" Mishca's cousin asked.

"Not sure," Mishca began.

Nurse Sue closed the doors and screamed for the nearest waiting room patient to bring over their chairs. There was a fuss, but the woman commanded them with ease. The person she yelled at had little time to think, so they acted. Bringing up a few chairs they propped them on the handles just so to make it hard for anyone on the opposite side to open. Odd. Mishca was starting to think this was no time for frozen thoughts. She eyed the front door and proceeded to whisper to her cousin and the other two to follow her out.

"Oh my god!" screamed one of her cousin's friends.

The chairs on the door did nothing to stop what came out. A man, or thing came crashing through the double doors with such ferocity that it broke the wood and metal frame. It sent the chairs flying to the other side of the room.

Nurse Sue ran as one of the waiting room patients trailed behind trying desperately to get away from whatever this thing was. As she ran, the patient was pushed down and fell in front of the door, scaring nurse Sue away and towards the nurse's station instead.

The others in the room screamed. Chaos it seemed and everything was going so fast it was as if time appeared to stop. Mishca then noticed the creature thing attack the male patient, the others either stood around screaming or grabbing the nearest object to fight. She decided to look around and saw the window the girls were near earlier. It was one of the only ways out, but so normal in size that it would take too long to get out. At this point she had wanted to hide. Maybe call the cops, or animal control. Hell, even the FBI!

That is when she took a real notice of it, that thing that came through the double doors. It had skin, but it was riddled with bumps and a wetness that seemed slick. Kind of when you go out for a run on a hot humid morning. His, or its arms were terribly long and had no hands or fingers. Its face was just, a blob of skin, bumpy skin. There was blood everywhere and for a moment she wasn't sure how the patient was being harmed. Then looking further she saw how he was being pulled apart. Each long arm was pulling at the man's body, taking large chunks away. That is when the room erupted with more screams and now frantic people in full fight mode. Some managed to hide under a small table.

Mishca took charge by grabbing the three girls and running to the nurse's station. It was no use. Nurse Sue had locked the door behind her, and the partition was sealed further with wood shutters they must use when they need to lock it up tight after hours. This wasn't going to work and so the window was the next option. She ran to it while more sounds, louder sounds, were coming from far away. It echoed deep and only grew.

"Mishca!" screamed her cousin.

Looking back she saw how a few more creatures or whatever they were standing in the room. People were running about trying to get to the front door, some were actively breaking into the nurse's station. No use, they had to get out and all those locations were shut tight. She ignored the coming terror and focused on opening the window. It was surprisingly easy. As she pulled it all the way up, she grabbed her cousin first. Practically pushing her out the girl screamed. For a moment Mishca thought about how unsafe it was inside, but what if something worse were out there? At this point, it didn't matter. Once the girl was out she grabbed another one. It took an incredible amount of will to help the others. She just wanted to get her family out safe and be done. However, she couldn't live with herself if she let anything else happen to the other two. They were just kids.

The light began to flicker and the emergency lights were visually blaring through the room. It gave everything a fiendish glow like a haunted house. As she was pushing the second girl out, the others must have come to some sense and noticed what they were doing. With death just ripping people apart, they ran towards her. One of the men pushed her away leaving her and the third girl behind. He was a hefty man and in no way could ever escape from that window.

It must have been luck, or just piss poor timing because one of the creatures grabbed on to him. Mishca looked through the room shrouded in darkness and bright emergency lights. There was little movement except people being killed. As the man screamed in agony, she grabbed the girl and attempted to climb over him and the creature to push her out the window. The girl felt stiff, like petrified wood just stuck in the ground. These precious little seconds wasted by her fear. As the man became silent it was now or never and Mishca made a choice. She stood on both of them and willed all her strength, but it wasn't enough. The window was too high and she was too damn short.

Just then she felt her cousin and the friend grab her arms and torso and pull her out. They were tiny girls but adrenaline had clearly kicked in. As they all fell from the window, the creature wasn't far behind. Barely able to breathe and with so much energy spent up to this point, Mishca still managed to get up, grab both girls and run around the building to the parking lot. As they ran, she hoped the creature would be too large to properly fit though the window. Regardless of that hopeful fact, she picked up the pace just in case she were wrong.

Driving was difficult. Her breathing was labored and the girls wouldn't stop crying. She wasn't even sure of where she was going. All of it seemed so unreal. Just one more night and she would have been gone. One more night and she would have avoided this. Whatever this was!

"Where's Ara?" asked her cousin.

"She's in the back," replied Mishca.

"No that's Taryn,"

"Look, we didn't have time. You saw what that thing was! How close it got to me! If I saved her I would have died!"

The two were silent. She didn't mean to sound so insensitive, so unkind. Not that she really cared. What a horrible thing to think of, but it couldn't be helped. She wanted to live.

The sky was dark and everything was still. She saw how the town was as lively as ever. It was as if no one knew what was happening, as if all they experienced wasn't real. That is until she saw someone without a face. It wasn't apparent at first, but freakishly long arms were a dead give away. Her cousin screeched and that is when Mishca knew, this was not just at the clinic. It was everywhere! No one seemed to notice until the first person was attacked. Chaos soon followed and Mishca was now weaving in and out of traffic to leave the area before more of those things appeared.

Before she could reach the street her aunt and uncle lived, a host of army trucks blocked their way. Looking around for another route, a man came onto their door and knocked loudly on the window. Afraid that this was another one of those creatures, Mishca began to floor it. That is when her cousin said they had on gas masks and army gear. Coming out of the car they were visually examined. Bright lights were shown in their eyes and their shirts moved up to see their torso.

Once Mishca was checked it was clear they were fine. So they were escorted onto a truck. Inside, there were others. Everything was quick and precise, as if the soldiers were use to this. Was there an attack? Had this happened before, but somewhere else? No one talked. And just like that, they were taken away.

During a moment of peace, Mishca's cousin finally noticed the pain radiating from her broken arm. The girl took refuge in her cousin's embrace as the truck drove over rough terrain. Looking around, it was hard to see the others inside. Darkness concealed their faces, which made Mishca nervous. She needed to see them, needed to know if any one of them were those monsters. This wasn't a time to relax, not when those things were everywhere.

A loud cough caught her off guard and startled a few others. Using her hearing to zero in on the source of the noise, she found herself looking to her left. She saw her cousin's friend, Taryn, holding her face. The kid was shaken up and probably frightened at the whole ordeal. A night where she should have been at a party with her crew turned into this. Feeling sorry for her, Mishca went to hold the girl. Peering into her face, she could see nothing. Was it the lack of light in the truck? Was her imagination running wild after her experience at the clinic? She couldn't be sure.

"Taryn…where's your face?" asked her cousin.

Feeling something odd, Mishca pushed the girl away violently into another passenger. Just as she did the girl screamed. The others moved about, nervous at what was unfolding in front of their eyes.

"Why did you push me?" the girl, Taryn, asked.

Feeling around for her phone Mishca attempted to turn on its flashlight feature. After fumbling for several long seconds, she saw with the intensity of the light that the girl did indeed have a face. Just as she was about to delve into embarrassment, the truck jerked about violently. Something or someone had careened into them. Losing her balance, the phone slid about the floor, illuminating the faces of the passengers. As she went to grab it, a long tentacle like thing slithered its way toward her. Screaming, she tried her best to stand. Feeling someone snatch her from behind, she avoided the long glistening thing.

"What's wrong?" asked her cousin.

That is when she looked. The two of them saw with clarity that standing there was a man. Light ignited his features from below, giving him an unnatural aura of white. They saw as his eyes turned into a mass lump of flesh. It absorbed his nose and mouth, along with his brows. All that was left was the slickness of his skin. Bumps protruded to the surface from beneath.

Everyone on their side of the truck saw it too and erupted with screams. Clawing at the sides of the truck, they tried to leave by burying themselves in metal. The creature was blocking the back of the truck and there was no other way to get by. Those that did were grabbed and just as quickly pulled apart.

Mishca thought about giving up, but then she decided to do something entirely different. Holding her cousin very tightly, and the other girl with a free arm, she instructed them to run once it was distracted and never stop running. Her cousin was beginning to argue when Mishca lunged at the creature. Pulling it to the side she felt her flesh rip like a doll being torn from its seams. The pain was sudden, sharp, but dulled in a moment. Her eyes became glossy and then, black. The final sound she heard was the voice of her cousin yelling,

"Mishca, no!"

CHAPTER 3

TAKE SHELTER

Day 1

The day was cool, brisk in all its somber tone. Serrie was surveying a building for her company. An old mall that had been abandoned for a few months. The supplies from some of the shops were still there, in storage. Times were rough and places — like the shops that lit up the sky with neon lights — were the first to go. This assignment was going to be a way for her to move up the ladder and possibly get a raise. Several of her colleagues were there.

The building was in good condition, although it had been built in the early eighties. Many of the winding corridors of the backrooms and halls led from one store to the other. A labyrinth of sorts. She got dizzy the first time around, but was able to get a layout before the first encounter. Should it even be called that? Attack was more like it. When her team left the back halls, they were at a stairwell. Straight ahead were large windows. From there they went up the stairs and saw, with unease, the entity that hovered in the sky. Formless but menacing nonetheless.

As everyone made their way upstairs she heard screams. Outside of the mall one of her colleagues was being, absorbed via his skin. The blur of it made her feel heady. Others were outside, just randoms on the street. Serrie got a bad feeling and needed to retreat. The car park was far and she didn't think she'd make it. Was it the fact that the mall was closer and she knew of a good hiding place? Perhaps. She couldn't just leave the others to die, so in a moment of sheer leadership, she ordered anyone around her to follow.

Serrie, three coworkers, and over a dozen other people, including children, made their way into the mall. The creature things followed. Her voice must have carried because she saw others trying to make their way into the mall. They were all scurrying about because they didn't know where to go, but she did. Down the stairs and into the only unlocked door leading to the backrooms. The winding labyrinth.

Day 42.

Quiet and foreboding as usual. Serrie was patrolling the hall alone. It was a common day. Wake up, drink some boiled water, eat a protein laden ration, then do your duty. Everyone had their duty, their purpose for the work. Her's was no different. If you had told her she'd be going down semi poor lit halls in a cold abandoned building's bunker, with a gun no doubt, she'd laugh her ass off. Funny how an office manager can go from that, to this.

"Serrie, you there," squeaked her walkie.

"Yeah, I'm here. What's up," she replied.

"Murphy's bum leg is actin' up again. Could you finish your round then head over to the botanist to retrieve her data?"

"Yeah."

Murphy and his fucked up leg again. Sure. That guy was a walking waste of space. Along with a few others. Useless and a detriment to the work. It was bad enough they had only twenty-three people. Five less from when they started. What made it worse was that they needed them all to keep to their duty in order to make it work, to survive. Murphy was not keeping up his end.

At the three quarters mark of her patrol, she eyed the layered planks of wood to the side that shielded the door frame. The small cracks were littered with paper. Not one area uncovered. Her heart raced and she had this feeling of getting more paper, add more to conceal the spaces that weren't there. Overkill she said to herself. It couldn't be helped. If even one piece wasn't there, if anyone saw what was on the other side…

"Hey Serrie," squeaked her walkie.

"Yeah," she replied.

"When you're done with the botanist, can you help Tam out with the electrics?"

She paused, annoyed at the amount of work she had to do. The work that was really somebody else's.

"Yeah," she said.

The botanist was far into the shelter. Her room was dark and damp. The floor was littered with dirt, hard packed soil from the actual ground beneath the building's original infrastructure. It was perfect for growing fresh vegetables. The issue was light. Since the beginning, they all were at a huge disadvantage. With the chaos happening so sudden and without mercy, any and all supplies they had were from the building itself. Even when hours turned into days, when no help came, some decided to venture out. Maybe gather nearby supplies until things got better. Back when they all thought things could get better. They've since come to the realization that it was all just a pipe dream.

"I'm here to get your report," said Serrie.

The botanist was a woman in her forties and the first to lay out plans of a long term stay. When it first happened she saw just how savage it all was. There was no going back to normal in that case. When she found this space in the lower level of the shelter, she was filled with joy for the first time in days. She was also in charge of water maintenance and the food distribution. Murphy was her helper of sorts. Was, is the operative word. That man was useless.

She had a name, but everyone just called her the botanist. It didn't bother her. She had a role, a duty and was very adept. There was a certain pride she got from talking about her work. Although she spent a large amount of time alone, doing this and that or whatever she did. Everyone trusted her so they kept their distance as long as they had fresh water to drink and nutritional food to eat.

Serrie was handed the report wrapped up in old newspaper. After trading pleasantries, she left to give them to the man on the other end of the walkie. Cutler was a gruff man, not really a leader, he wasn't military. However, the way he ran things you'd swear he did a tour some time in his life. Guess he always wanted that sort of glory and this hell of a situation was the only way he was going to get it.

"Thanks Serrie," he said as she handed him the report.

Cutler unwrapped it as she looked on. She wanted to tell him to get someone else to do such stupid things like get papers. Maybe one of those kids that did nothing else but eat, drink, and wander around. The idea of saying something and nothing bounced around her mind like a game of ping pong when she saw his eyes grow after reading the report. He closed the papers, and for a moment he looked like he was in mourning.

"Bad news?" she asked.

She'd hate to admit it, but she was intrigued. What had the botanist wrote that made him react in this manner? He eyed her, scrutinizing why she was still there. However, he didn't say anything. After some time thinking, he must have decided to let her in the loop.

"We have limited supplies," he said.

"No shit," she replied.

Really? Limited supplies was common place. The fact that they had anything was a testament of luck. Sheer luck at that. He explained that the food and few supplies they were able to procure from that dangerous mission a month ago was dwindling. They'd have to go out again. The thought of going outside, out there with them, was not just dangerous, but impossible.

"The last time, the only time we went out there, we lost five people! Five! And how many did we send that first time?" Serrie said.

"Seven," he replied.

"Out of seven, only two came back. And they still aren't over it!" she said practically screaming.

Staring at the man as he let out a gruff breath, she let his words weigh on her. Needing some time to think she felt her body move her out into the hall. It was just one bad disaster after the other. Sitting on the floor she heard the pitter patter of footsteps running toward her. Dan was a precocious kid. He did what he was told to a fault. One thing he did well was keep an eye on the others and report anything wrong.

"Let me guess, someone took an extra ration?" Serrie said.

"Not today," Dan said "we were all going around the halls when we came to that dead end. Dallas wanted to look in the cracks. He kept teasing everyone to look."

When Dan said we, he meant the kids. There were only five. Some were as young as seven while Dallas was the oldest at thirteen. He was a pain, but he was just a kid. Serrie wanted to slap him a few times, but realized early on how scared he was. His father had been one of the people who went to find supplies and didn't come back. This was his little way of controlling something, anything to feel; to feel powerful and not weak. She reluctantly stood on her feet and went to the storage rooms where many of them set up camp.

Dallas was sitting around with the others, telling them a story. It must have been a scary one because they all looked frightened, but listened with awe. Serrie would have waited until he was finished, she wanted to talk herself out of dealing with the little pain. He noticed her almost immediately. Together in the hall she had a heart to heart talk with the kid.

"You know they are scared right?" she began, "that we are all scared, even the adults."

"What's this even about?" he replied, trying to play coy.

"Look, you want to scare everyone and cause trouble, fine. But you'll find yourself out of here if that's the case. You can be great you know. A leader, someone that can do some real good. But you choose to be worthless. Choose better!"

Just like that she was done. It was harsh, but she didn't care if she hurt his feelings. Things were not going well with the food running low. She had no time to be gentle or understanding. He either got the full picture or not.

"Sorry," he said as she walked away. She didn't look back.

Day and night had no meaning where they were. With no windows, no way of seeing anything of the outside world, they simply had to listen to their bodies to know when it was time to rest. Serrie had a difficult time with this as her anxiety kept her from sleep most days. That first week, no one slept. They had to board up the doors leading to stores and stairwells to keep the things out. Those creepy creatures that were all different in their forms. While some were merely blurs, the ones that took solid shapes were the most dangerous. Anyone who saw those were, for the lack of better words, different. Their eyes taking on a whitish glow. Maybe they had lost five people when they went to fetch more supplies, but they lost others before that when they simply looked at those, things.

When Serrie had managed to fall asleep, she was plagued by nightmarish visions. The depths of which were so real, so terrible, that she woke in cold sweats. Fearing she might be going insane, she tied herself up to keep from turning into the ones who had their eyes whired out. To say that she wasn't sleep deprived and paranoid was a farce. Everything around her was a threat and she had treated it just the same. Even Dallas. That is why she had been so hardened, so cold. This was how everyone was, it was their way of surviving, living to another day. A day that was quickly shortening due to the limited resources. She buried her head in her pillow and screamed.

An unbearable silence deafened her to wake. Strange, like a television turning on for the first time in hours. That odd sensation of static lingering in the ears. Serrie had a bad feeling, like some hidden thing lurking in her spine. She tingled with sensation that left her flesh covered in heat bumps. Opening her mouth to say something, she couldn't. The sudden fear that froze her, limited her breath. Trying so hard to inhale, she gasped. Taking no comfort in the effort, she moved her arms about wildly. She began to think about all the terrible things that could happen, things she couldn't see. Was it here? Was she dying? Was she being, absorbed? Nothing could release her from this foreboding feeling. Then finally, she heard a voice.

"Serrie," it said.

She closed her eyes, and at once she was in the storage room, able to move once again. Jolting up she gave a sharp cry that made her sound younger than what she was.

"Serrie?" it said once more.

She looked all around her to find the person who belonged to the voice, but could not. Was she going mad? Had this all been a dream, or even a night terror? She had never had one to know for sure. It felt real, she didn't feel like she was dreaming.

"Serrie!" it said again.

A sudden pull ached at her chest, moving her forward. Faint whispers could be heard, almost inaudible. She strained to hear it, but the force that was making her go was impossible to resist. From that moment, a formless creature began to take shape and that is when she heard her voice. It was so intense that for several moments she doubted it came from herself. Then she opened her eyes, and was surrounded by Tam and the others.

"Shit Serrie! You near gave us all a heart attack!" said Tam.

He was practically heaving as if he were running far past his own endurance. Were her cries truly that gut wrenched that it echoed through the halls? For a brief moment she took in the relief of seeing someone she knew. Then quickly she lowered her eyes, embarrassed at her actions.

"You okay?" he asked.

From around her she saw several of the others, looking on with concern, a few, contempt. Sleep was hard to get, and when someone managed, being jolted awake for a nonemergency was beyond irritating. When everyone realized that all was fine, they left, leaving her there with Tam. From the door, the botanist stood with just half her face being seen from the henge. Quietly, she left too.

❖

The next morning, or whatever time it was, Serrie made her way to Cutler. He was cleaning some weapons, preparing for another excursion. A suicide mission in her eyes. He didn't need to look up to know it was her. Over time, with their small population, everyone had a certain thing about them that was distinct. Dan had his pitter patter of steps like he was always ready to go, the botanist had her dripping plants, or dripping parts of her clothing, even Dallas had a certain way of walking that was entirely his own.

Standing by Cutler she began to talk, but he cut her off.

"We go in two days."

"I see," Serrie replied.

Her tongue rolled around her mouth trying to keep her dismay, her anger, and despair at bay. It was no use, she had to say something. Just when she released her tongue, he cut her off again.

"You think we can stay here forever?" he asked "we got kids here, food running low, and we just can't go on like this."

"So we go out there? And what? Risk dying, or whatever those things do to people?" she said.

"You got another idea?" he asked.

Throughout their conversation, Cutler kept on cleaning the weapons. She eyed him callously, but she couldn't help but think, he was right. He gave her a list of supplies they needed and who to bring on their mission. This was not going to go well.

In the large storage room they all gathered, including the children. Serrie announced who would be going on their little trip and immediately the chaos began. One woman cried while another person rolled his eyes with contempt. It was when she announced that the food was running low that they all stood at attention. Their eyes became downcast and forlorn. She hated that she had to give everyone the bad news. After the air was filled with despair of what they needed to do, Cutler made his way in with the weapons. Giving each of the people their share, he took over the conversation. Over and over they went through the plan. It was bad enough that anyone had to leave their security of concealment into that abyss of death outside. What made it worse was that Serrie was one of the poor unfortunates that had to go too.

The two days passed with very quick succession. Almost too quick, as if time was speeding up. If it had been any other day, time would be slow, to an almost unbearable halt. Now it was the day they all dreaded. Going over the plan one more time, Serrie looked around at their group. It was her, Tam, Samantha, Ricki and Cutler. She wondered how many would make it back this time and if they would actually find anything at all. The prospect looked frighteningly dreadful.

From the door they stood. The botanist and Dallas were there to send them off and be a sort of line of defense waiting for their return. They would only open the door when one of them was present. Any other noise was rightfully shut out. They also took a walkie, but only in absolute emergency. To use it outside was just inviting death to take you. Serrie gathered up her unease and opened the door leading to the stairwell. As it opened, everyone braced for what was on the other side. Cutler was next to Serrie and even his breath had gone cold, readying himself for a battle. A war that he was bound to lose.

Nothing was there, and so they walked, cautiously up into the mall. Peaking behind corners they were careful not to look directly at any one thing. The sky from the windows was ashen gray. Serrie hadn't breathed air, real air since the day it happened. Even this small relief was tainted by the idea that the very atmosphere they breathed was possibly toxic. Whatever had happened weeks ago was something no one could have ever predicted. They knew little about it and being out in the open could very well lead to their demise. It filled her thoughts and overtook her senses, mainly her eyes. She bumped stupidly into a table, knocking over a few items.

Crash! Everyone froze, gripped their weapons and waited for something. Nothing came. Cutler looked back to see Serrie with wide eyes. Her skin felt hot from the embarrassment. What could he expect since she didn't even want to be here. The group continued throughout the store and from there, the rest of the mall. It was eerily silent, so much so that their quiet footsteps were easy to hear as well as their shallowed breaths. Everyone was on high alert, but the mall remained quaint as if nothing were wrong.

Cutler lead the group to a door at the very end of the complex. From the first day they knew the only supplies they could use were either in the storage spaces where they took shelter, or outside of the actual mall. It meant that the mall itself was mostly, if not, completely empty. Liminal space had been the look of the mall since its closing prior to all of this. It left it appearing wrong, even before those things showed up. Very few stores had items inside, which meant that all the other spaces were left with nothing. The air of despair was stifling, as if the derelict state of the the mall itself had brought about the apocalypse. What a frightening thought.

Standing by the glass doors, they all looked outside. It was easy to be tempted by the urge to go back. To not risk one's own life for little to nothing. Cutler whispered to everyone that they had to keep focus and stay on their game. Tam nodded and looked over at the others as they followed suit. Serrie was not ready, but going back alone was not exactly a decent option either. They opened the doors and made their way into the street. None of them could have foreseen the chaos they saw. Only those that had died before and the two that came back had seen the aftermath of the carnage. Putrid bodies were strewn about the streets. Discarded like worn clothes. The cars vacant, one door held ajar. The lights were on in some stores. For some odd reason, the power grid had not gone completely off. This gave Serrie a sense that out there, somewhere, this chaos had not reached the rest of the world.

A sound from the distance gathered everyone's attention. They were careful not to look at it directly, for fear of what they might see. Cutler motioned for everyone to follow him to a set of cars to hide. As the others took note, Serrie had a strange sensation on her flesh. For a moment she mistook it for fear, perhaps gooseflesh popping up. It felt so odd, then suddenly it hurt! She turned only to see a blur of something, nothing, but it was there! Not certain if it was her own body that had moved her, or Tam, but she was being pulled away. The sound of guns and even a flare had been thrown at the creature.

Her body became limp and as she struggled to stay awake, she felt the heavy footsteps and deep breaths of Tam as he ran frantically. The sky above was still dark, clouded and awfully still. Then it became the ceiling of the mall. They were going back to the shelter. She heard no other footsteps. Upon coming to the door, Tam kicked the door violently. There were sounds coming from behind and all at once her senses became clear. The pain of her flesh followed as if it had been on mute, then resumed with no delay.

Seconds appeared as minutes until finally they were let inside. From there, chaos. People crying and breathing heavily. Arguments ensued. Serrie was taken to a storage room reserved for medical use. A medical student named Elam worked on her skin. He insisted she was going to be fine, but his eyes betrayed him. The botanist came at once and took over. It was strange for her to be so invested. This was not her expertise. Elam didn't even seem to notice and took her orders without hesitation. They worked on her until she passed out.

Awake after however much time passed, Serrie stared at the ceiling. The room was dimly lit and smelled of mold. She wanted to turn, to get up, but her skin still felt odd. Moving her hands she felt the bandages wrapped around her body. It didn't seem to end. Fearful that she was truly scarred, she forced herself to sit up. It was useless, as her arms were too weak. She lay still for several minutes and began to panic as she heard heavy breathing. Most of the room was shrouded in darkness, so she couldn't pin point the origin of the sound. Then her anxiety shot up when she thought this might be a dream, the odd visions she was so use to seeing when she slept. Was this another bout of a frightful encounter with the sandman?

Opening her mouth, she tried to call for help. To her relief, she could. She screamed, when suddenly the door swung open. It was hard to see who it was, the form was indistinct. When it moved, she knew exactly who had entered, the botanist. The woman stood over Serrie and told her to keep quiet. Confused and riddled with questions, Serrie tried to ask why she was here. The botanist said nothing more and left. Serrie took the time to feel around for something, anything that she could use. She wasn't even sure why it seemed important, but she couldn't just lay there doing nothing.

When the heavy breathing resumed, she was reminded of her original fear upon waking up. Someone or something was in the room with her. Now she looked around and tried to eye the source of the light. It wasn't much, but it would be enough to use in order to find out what was in the room with her. Feeling around again, she used her arms to drag herself. The light was perched up on something, a table she presumed. Serrie had a tough time moving and felt the bandages being pulled with every thrust. It was exhausting and painful. Then she froze as she felt a sharp tear. Consumed in an instant with unbearable pain, she screamed!

The door opened again and inside came the botanist. To Serrie's surprise, the woman moved her about with ease. Then she walked away and in came a burst of light. It revealed a derelict storage room that Serrie had never seen. Her eyes had a hard time adjusting as the botanist moved her body around and removed the bandage that had come undone. Fighting through the pain of the light and the pain of her skin, Serrie looked around as best she could to find the source of the heavy breathing. To her dismay and utter shock, she saw what appeared to be a decrepit bundle of flesh. It looked decayed and had a shimmering slickness. As her eyes adjusted more, she saw that it had a face. Blinking back several times Serrie came to the realization that this lump of festering flesh was none other than Murphy!

She immediately forgot about her skin that pained her so and tried desperately to stand on her own. Her legs weren't moving. Looking down she saw how they were bandaged too. What was supposed to be there was much too short. As if most of her legs were simply not there. Serrie eyed the botanist who gave her a discrete smile. Getting ready to scream, the botanist had taken a bandage and wrapped it around Serrie's mouth silencing her at once. Finding it difficult to breathe, she went to remove the bandages, only for her hands to be tied up like mittens.

"You make a sound, I bound you down," said the botanist.

The woman stood, and as Serrie trembled with the reality of her situation, the botanist made her way around the room. Boxes used for their food supplies and water were everywhere. A deepening dread sunk Serrie's heart. The lights went off and from there, the botanist's steps faded until the door closed behind her.

CHAPTER 4

DEAR SOLDIER

Artie was a man who saw his purpose from the moment he was a child. Taking after his father, grandfather, and great-grandfather, he joined the army. Freshly out of high school, he trained on a base several miles from his home. It was what he enjoyed, what he knew and everyone accepted his choice. As much as it pleased him to serve, it all went terribly wrong after he was deployed for the first time. His first real mission had been a bust. With all his training and effort, it was as if his body couldn't take the shock of it all. The chaos that consumed the air around him. He was found not far from the site, holding his head and battling a bout of sickness.

When he woke on the hospital bed, he insisted he was alright. Lying to the doctors, his body told the truth. He was not fit for combat. When he was returned home and given other options, he just couldn't do it. His purpose was there, in front of him, but his condition kept it out of reach. Days and weeks went by, but nothing could soothe his despair. Feeling intense anger at his own body for betraying him, he succumbed to other means. This only worsened his condition and ruined any alternative prospects for that military life. The life he so badly needed.

It was a cold damp day when he was visited by a friend. Someone else, a brother of sorts, who had joined the military at the same time. Only, he was still there and Artie was not. He missed his old life and old friends, so he wasn't quick to dismiss him; although jealousy was always on the tip of his mind.

"I see you're looking better," his friend said.

His eyes wandered around the mess of a home, Artie's home. The two sat on the couch, the only places not covered in clothes, trash, or sticky liquids. As a friend, he insisted Artie see a professional. Someone to take him out of his rut. It was just disastrous since he felt no way out of this dilemma. Staring at the floor, Artie tried to listen, but all he could think about was his failure and need to be great. That is when the mood shifted and his friend abruptly stood.

"I get it. You got men in your life who all have stories from the military. And now you're breaking that streak. It isn't your fault. But this," his friend paused and motioned around the room "this is your fault. You may not be able to be in combat and your behavior may have ruined any future career, but there's other ways to serve your country."

Artie was ready to vent his frustration when the last words caught his attention.

"What way?" asked Artie.

His friend gave him a card. It only had a number and nothing more. Being vague, the friend only said that it was private contract work for former military.

Artie dismissed it and said he wouldn't be eligible. The friend then sat next to him and said,

"With the work they do, they'll bend the rules."

To be apart of whatever this new job was, Artie had to seek help. He had to get ready to work. That meant cleaning up his place, himself, and getting right in the head. After a few months, he was somewhat ready. It had been so long since he held a stable job, or felt truly useful that he doubted how things would go. Even as he took a plane all the way across the country and was driven over a hundred miles, he wasn't sure he could do this.

The men in the car were silent and only stated that he would know more when they arrived. Artie had some hesitation, but his friend had connected him, so it wasn't like it was a total scam. He had heard stories of military men going into the private sector and making money. It couldn't be all bad.

The air smelled dry and filled with sand. Artie clenched his hands to rid his body of anxiety. He had been getting help and taking his medication he was prescribed, but the time he got help to now was too soon. Perhaps he wouldn't be able to do the job. It was a terrible thought. Breathing in and out, he moved passed the intrusive frustration he felt and closed his eyes to calm his mind.

Finally arriving at the base, he looked with awe as they traversed underground. It was frighteningly deep. The air cooled tremendously and for the first time in months, Artie felt some form of relief. He was able to relax. When the car stopped Artie was greeted by a man named Ivan. He was a tall man who clearly had strong military training just based on his physique alone. Ivan didn't smile, but his gentle nature seemed nice. Artie saw the dark dingy underground world where he would be working. There were lights, but the closeness of everything was a stark difference to the open spaces of the ground above. He looked at this man Ivan and though, perhaps his luck could change.

Over the course of ten weeks, Artie had found his calling. His job was simple, patrol the corridors, while carrying a gun, do some light maintenance, and keep his room tidy. It was easy work, but it was work. He had a gun again and responsibilities. It was all he ever wanted. The men he worked with were kind enough. They would talk about their lives and the paths that led them to this base, but something about their demeanor was off. Whenever the conversation about what went on at this place came up, they would steer the conversation somewhere else. Then they'd keep talking as if the question had never been asked. It was odd.

Artie had made friends, but he truly enjoyed working with Ivan. The man reminded him of his father. Although stern and focused, he was kind and had an air of respectability. It was comforting, especially since he had a falling out with his own dad after his discharge from the military. His failures couldn't be helped and his father never truly forgave him for it. Ivan on the other hand had learned of Artie's past and accepted him for who he was; this included what he couldn't control.

After more time went, Artie was assigned a new position. To patrol the corridors of the lower level. Five stories down, the air chilled to an unbearable frost. He was startled at the bright intensity, yet frigid atmosphere. There he would do what he had always done, but after his shift, he would go into decontamination. His new assignment would also require him to bunk at this lower level, this frozen tundra of a place. Artie wasn't upset, in fact, he saw this as an opportunity to improve his position. His enthusiasm was being lost on the new group of men he met.

Unlike his fellow coworkers five stories up, the men here were distant. No one talked, no one smiled, and everyone seemed painfully focused. Perhaps it was the decontamination they underwent after each shift that kept their attention at full. Whatever the reason, Artie tried to not let it interfere with his glee of moving up in this new profession.

The days melted into each other as Artie tried to maintain his calm. Being that no one talked, and little information was given about why they were there, Artie found it difficult to know the purpose of it all. Things were no different up there, but below, his curiosity was beginning to nip away at his mind. It unnerved him how everyone seemed, for the lack of better words, ready. As if at any moment things could go wrong. Or perhaps they have and that is why he had been assigned. Try as he might to not let his curiosity stab his mind, it could be helped. There was something odd about this level. He could sense it.

On one of his rounds, he was so focused on what ifs and thoughts, that he went further into a corridor that was outside of his patrol. When he realized this was not his assigned area, he began to turn around. That is when he spotted the door. It was a large thing. It appeared caked into the wall and sealed at the henges. Throughout his time in this underground, he never saw anyone working, only men like him patrolling. Whatever this place was used for, maybe it was behind this door. The thought in his head told him to go back to his patrol, but his curiosity had finally won.

Looking around to spot any cameras, he inched his way to the door. Half expecting to hear scientists, or even gears and machines, he was taken aback by a woman's voice. In normal circumstances it wouldn't have been anything out of sorts, but what alarmed him was that she spoke directly to his presence.

"Who is there?" she asked.

Afraid to out himself and ruin his position at this new job, he remained silent. Shaking, he wondered how she knew he was there. His steps made no noise, and the thickness of the door seemed to mute any sounds she could have heard. He wasn't even sure how he was hearing her at all.

"I know you're there," she said.

Now certain that there were cameras, he had a decision to make. Leave now and pretend he heard nothing, or admit his failure and feed his curiosity. The thoughts were rupturing his mind so much that he closed his eyes to calm himself.

"What's your name?" she asked.

"I'm not supposed to talk to you," Artie replied.

There was a pause, as if she contemplated his answer.

"Who told you not to?" she asked.

"No one," Artie said, half annoyed that he was in this predicament in the first place. He continued despite himself, "I just don't think it's a good idea."

"Why?" she asked.

"Because that is not my job."

"What is your job?"

"I patrol the corridors."

"Sounds boring."

What an odd thing to say, he thought to himself. Who was she? He had to know.

"It's loads more fun than what you do," he said.

"You see me?"

"No, I can't. But I assume you are more bored than me."

"How so?"

"Because if you weren't, you wouldn't be talking to me."

She began to laugh, startling him. He thought that the door might muffle her, but it was as if there was no door there. Her voice was so clear, so distinct. He continued on, his curiosity leading him recklessly.

"What's your name?" she asked.

If she were asking, then that meant she couldn't see him. If she did, maybe she'd had checked his file. Surely the people who worked here would know of him. Or maybe she hadn't checked yet. He could get out of this if he were smart. If only he were smart.

"What are you doing behind that door?" he asked, trying to change the subject.

"Nothing at all," she said, not missing a beat.

"Well, I should be getting back," he said.

"Bye," she replied.

That night he lay in bed thinking about the mysterious woman on the other side of the door. Who she could be, what she was really doing, and if he would get in trouble. When morning came and no one had spoken to him about his conversation, he was relieved. His curiosity was sparked again at the thought of speaking to her once more. He liked his new job, but the atmosphere of this lower level was sucking him dry. He needed to speak with someone, to have interactions, to do something other than patrol all day. During his shift he made his way to that corridor and to the door. All the while, he checked his surroundings, half expecting to get caught.

"You're back?" she asked.

"Yes. It's me," he replied.

"Oh, good! How was your patrol?"

"Usual."

"Sounds boring as usual."

"It is."

The days continued this way. Artie going through the corridors as instructed. Then he would find his way to that particular door and speak with the woman. Their conversations were brief, never lasting more than a few minutes at a time. She was easy to talk to, even when he let personal things slip, like his condition, his short term military service, and general unhappiness. The woman was a comfort he never could have foreseen. Even if they never truly met face to face, it was nice to speak with someone and for them to listen.

During meal time he ate solemnly, counting down the time he would be on patrol again, to speak with her. Time began to blur and soon he found himself drunk on their interactions. Now their conversations lasted longer, grew more personal. Although, she kept her life a secret. It was okay, perhaps she wasn't ready. He could be patient. Even when days turned into weeks, he felt a quaint happiness that he hadn't felt in a long time. Artie felt rather foolish falling for someone he technically didn't really know.

All was right when he noticed a few odd stares from the others. They never said anything, but their cold looks were unpleasant. Could they know? Was he being careless spending thirty minutes talking about nothing to someone behind a door? Would he lose his job? A nagging feeling rose in him whenever he went on patrol now. Was he being followed? It became too much one day during meal time. Artie abruptly stood and when all eyes were on him, he simply walked to his bunk. His paranoia was getting to him and he needed her. When he went on patrol, he sped up just to get to her faster.

"I think they know," he said.

"I don't think so," she replied.

"How do you know?"

"Because you're the only one who ever comes here."

"Is that true?"

"I think. No one ever speaks to me. Then again, I don't speak to anyone other than you."

Artie felt a splash of relief at being the only one she spoke to. It was a good feeling to know their friendship was just between them. Odd as the whole thing was, it was nice to have something special. Suddenly he shook his head. What disastrous thoughts. It was wrong. The whole ordeal. He was being stupid and risking everything. Without saying goodbye, he left her, all the while she called out to him.

During the decontamination, the tech that processed him looked up. Without saying much, Artie was escorted to another room. He felt like he was in prison or at the very least, sent to the principal's office. As he waited he thought of his actions for the past few weeks. If they were going to fire him he'd surely accept it. Perhaps punishing himself for being so daft.

The door opened and with surprise, Artie saw Ivan. He hadn't seen the man in so long that a smile crept up his face. Ivan didn't reciprocate. The man sat and opened up a file. Reading quietly, Artie sat up strong, hoping to not let the disappointment of loosing his job show on his face. Ivan then spoke with a crossness he had never heard.

"How long have you interacted with it?" Ivan asked.

"It?" Artie said.

"What does it say?" Ivan asked.

"Sir? I don't understand. You mean the woman behind that door?" Artie asked, very much lost within this conversation.

Ivan looked up and pierced him with cold eyes.

"How long have you interacted with it?" Ivan asked again.

"A few weeks. And she is not an it. She's a person," Artie responded.

Artie tried to think of how anyone found out. Then he realized that he had just come from decontamination. Perhaps there was something in those results. Maybe there was something in that corridor and that is why no one patrolled it. He felt himself sinking into sudden despair when Ivan's voice brought him back.

"What does it say?" Ivan asked. His tone more forceful.

Artie took a deep breath and answered honestly.

"We talk about me mostly. I don't know anything about her," Artie said.

He felt unbearably stupid having told all of his business to a stranger just to lose it all. In his mind, it would have been worth it if he could at least see her once. Ivan's face showed no interest, only contempt. Artie then thought of how Ivan had addressed the woman, calling her an it. What was that about? He felt an overwhelming urgency to ask.

"Why do you call her, it?"

Ivan closed the file. "You will be moved up to the upper level and discharged shortly after your debriefing."

Just like that, Artie was out. Crestfallen, he sunk into his chair, his body betraying the stoic presence he had sought with so much effort to exude. When Ivan left, two men came for Artie. They escorted him to his bunk. In the morning, he would be moved to the upper level. He had all night to ponder his shortcomings.

It must have been late because there was a deafening silence. Artie rose from his bed; he hadn't taken a moment of sleep. Feeling the weight of all his decisions, he decided to make one last poor choice. He'd find out who that woman was and why he had lost his job. During the day it was easy to see others on patrol, but in the peak of night, there were very little numbers. It was easy to go past them and into the area of his former patrol. From there, he walked, each step out pacing the last. His mind was a flutter of anger, guilt, and shame. These feelings felt so foreign because for a time in a long while, he had actually accomplished something. Now he was back to where it began and all the negativity was brought back with full vengeance.

Then he saw that door, and the memories of his conversations flooded his mind, making him sick with nostalgia. As before, she noticed his presence. Something that didn't bother him much, was now filling him with unease. Ivan had referred to her as an it. Was this because she knew of his presence through a thick door?

"Hi soldier," she said. Her voice sounded sweet like a sugar coated sickle.

He now knew there was something odd about her. This made it easier to confront her; probe her for answers.

"What are you?" he asked.

"A person, same as you," she said.

"How can you know I'm here?"

"I just know."

"My superior, Ivan, called you an it."

She was silent. The minutes going on an uncomfortable amount of time.

"What's your name?" he finally asked.

"If I told you, would you help me?" she asked.

The idea intrigued him. However, the secrecy was overwhelming. He couldn't trust her, but the others were also less informative. A decision to help someone he knew, or the people that he worked with was difficult. For so long he wanted to have a place. Now that he had it, would he ruin it to help someone who was referred to as an it? Sitting down, he pondered on this request. A simple, yet disastrous one. She must have understood his trouble, because she was quiet once more.

"Tell me everything and I'll see," he responded.

"My name is Eve and I am a prisoner here," she began "they've sealed me in, but on another wall, they made it so that I can receive food. It is very little and they won't let me out."

Such an accusation. Artie was disturbed, and he hated himself for believing her. Why would they lock up a random woman. He wanted, no, needed more answers.

"Why would they lock you here?" he asked.

"I was taken here and they've done experiments on me. I don't know why. I can't see myself," she said.

Her voice cracked and he could visually see her tears in his mind. Artie looked at the door and saw that there was no way of getting in that way. He thought about what she said about the other wall that could open. Was there another way inside? He had been through many of the corridors and couldn't understand where the wall on the other side of her prison could be located. He stood and said he'd talk to Ivan. She quickly screamed a haunting no. Artie then leaned against a wall. If she were a victim of experimentation, surely this was why no one truly knew what went on and why all the men here were discharged from the military. They needed men like him. Men without a future, who had been lost and needed a way back into their former roles. Men who could be quiet and not ask questions. Men like himself. He felt terribly ashamed that he hadn't asked more questions. That he went along with walking down corridors without a care. Was he complicit in what was happening to Eve?

"What will you do?" she asked.

Artie was ready to make a decision. He wasn't certain if he'd regret it, but he knew that in this very moment, it needed to be done.

It was an hour before dawn and the amount of patrols would increase. Artie had his bag with the items. It took him some time to work on it and was a bit heavy. His body drooped to the side. He would compensate for this by forcing his body to lean the other way. As the time kept moving, he began to hear the bustling sound of men waking and getting ready for the day. Ivan would also be on his way to retrieve him. He had to act fast, increase his speed.

Making his way to the corridor — Eve's prison — he heard someone in the distance. Was someone calling his name? He couldn't be bothered to look. Practically running, he found her sealed door and began removing the item from his bag. Homemade, it had to work. The sound of the voice was louder, more distinct. It was another one of his colleagues and he was in fact saying his name.

Artie's fingers struggled with the inherent fear of what would become of him once they knew what he had done. That is, if everything went as planned. The voices were growing louder and Ivan could be heard as well. With the last of it set, Artie told Eve to back away as far as she could from the door. He stood some feet away. From the distance he saw several men. Now was the time to act. Pressing the trigger, a spark of a brilliant flash bathed the walls with a sound so deep it pained his eardrums. Falling to the floor, Artie was hit with a wave of nausea and vertigo. He couldn't orient himself and held his ears tight. The deafening silence with distant ringing was so palpable that he had to fight himself to keep conscious.

All around him was dust and chunks of where parts of the walls had been. Light fixtures hung from wires. He immediately began to think, how powerful did he make it? The thought was obliterated when he saw the dark opening where Eve's prison door once stood. Straining his eyes to see her, he felt sick when he thought of her possibly being hurt from the blast. Trying and failing to make himself stand, his feelings worsened. The explosion had triggered his condition. As he lay frozen in his own body, a terrible sight emerged.

Eve was not Eve, but something else of another form came from her door. This slick wet looking thing slithered out. Large and imposing, it loomed over Artie. From his condition and his terrified state, he couldn't see it properly. It surely was an it as Ivan had said it was. For a moment he thought he may have let out some other creature due to the large blast. That is, until it spoke.

With minor hearing loss from the explosion, he couldn't understand, but he was certain that it was her voice. An odd sensation overcame him. The creature and the surroundings had blurred to an almost impossible degree that he thought he was going blind. He felt cold. Its voice, her voice, lingered in his ear until he heard nothing and took his final breath.